The Easter Ribbit

To Jane, Margaret, and Cole Chardiet,
with all my love
— B.C.

To Lindsey, Sophia, and Marcus
— C.M.

ISBN 0-590-10072-6

10 9 8 7 6 5 4   8 9/9 0/0 01 02

Printed in the U.S.A.   24
First printing, February 1998

The Easter Ribbit

by Bernice Chardiet
Illustrated by Charles Micucci

SCHOLASTIC INC.
Cartwheel ·B·O·O·K·S·®
New York   Toronto   London   Auckland   Sydney

Easter was coming. The bunnies were very busy making pretty Easter baskets, carrying jelly beans, and painting eggs.

Froggie watched them from the pond.
Sometimes he wished he were a rabbit.
They seemed to be having so much fun.

Hmmm! Maybe he could convince Turtle to let him paint her eggs before they hatched.

Froggie quickly ran to the beach. Turtle was there covering her eggs with sand.

"Ribbit! Ribbit!" Froggie called to Turtle. "It's almost Easter! May I paint your eggs?"

"Keep quiet!" Turtle warned. "Can't you see I'm trying to hide them? If you were to paint them, every bird in the forest would see my eggs and eat them before the babies could hatch and crawl to the water. Go back to your log and stop bothering me!"

Froggie walked sadly to his favorite hollow log near the rabbit tree and crawled inside. After a long time of feeling sorry for himself, he fell asleep and had a dream.

In the dream he was an Easter Ribbit—not quite a rabbit but not a frog either. He was rushing through the high grass to deliver Easter baskets to all the children. The baskets were full of things that Froggie loved: jelly beans, lollipops, flies, tiny fish eggs, seaweed bars, and delicious mosquitoes, too.

Suddenly a terrible noise woke Froggie.
He opened his eyes and peeked out of the log.

The Chief Easter Bunny had just landed in a helicopter. He was carrying armfuls of lists of all the children who needed Easter presents. Mrs. Rabbit and all of her assistants came running out to greet him.

"You are doing a wonderful job!" said the Chief. "But we need more helpers! Can you handle an extra load of deliveries?"

"Oh, dear," said Mrs. Rabbit. "We don't have enough bunnies to deliver the baskets! Flossie and Fernie caught colds last night and I'm afraid they are running fevers. And Hubert and Henry hurt their feet squeezing under a fence. They can't run until next week. What will we do?"

"Advertise!" said the Chief Easter Bunny.

"Call Mrs. Duck's Employment Agency. She can fly over the woods and drop ads for the position *tonight*! Mrs. Duck's a quack but she may be able to help us."

"All right," said Mrs. Rabbit. "We'll do our best!"

Mrs. Duck was sound asleep when Mrs. Rabbit called, but she woke up and wrote the ad anyway. Unfortunately, Mrs. Duck was very nearsighted and didn't see her spelling mistake. Instead of writing an ad for an Easter Rabbit, she had written an ad for an Easter *Ribbit*.

One of the ads landed on Froggie's log. Froggie saw it as soon as he woke up the next morning. "An Easter Ribbit?" said Froggie. "That's me!" It was his dream come true! Quickly, he wrote down Mrs. Duck's address and ran to the employment office.

Although she couldn't see well, Mrs. Duck suspected that she was looking at a frog. Nevertheless, Froggie was the only client who had come into her office for a very long time, and there wasn't a rabbit in sight.

HELP
WANTED
EASTER
RIBBIT

Mrs. Duck ran to her storage room and cut out a big pair of paper bunny ears. She tied them on Froggie's head. Then Mrs. Duck pasted a big cotton ball on Froggie to make a rabbit's tail.

Froggie was divinely happy. He ran to Mrs. Rabbit's tree right away.

Mrs. Rabbit and all her assistants were working feverishly to color new eggs and fill new baskets. Glancing quickly at Froggie's big, floppy ears, Mrs. Rabbit didn't notice that he was an Easter Ribbit — and not an Easter Rabbit. She pointed to a tall tower of Easter baskets outside the back door and told Froggie to start his deliveries.

Froggie looked up at the baskets. "Ribbit!" he gasped. "I'll never be able to deliver all of these by Easter!"

There was only one thing to do. Quickly, he hopped down to the pond. Ribbiting as loudly as he could, Froggie called for all of his friends and relatives to come and help him. Soon a crowd of frogs of all shapes and sizes leapfrogged to pick up the baskets stacked behind Mrs. Rabbit's tree.

And if you had been anywhere near Froggie's log at the crack of dawn on Easter morning, you would have seen them marching through the meadow to deliver the Easter baskets to the children. And at the head of the parade was Froggie, ribbiting a happy song.

F R O G G I E ' S

I'm a froggie in a hurry,

And I've really got to scurry

Before the sun comes up.

While all the kids are sleeping,

I'll be hopping, sprinting, leaping.

I'm as happy as a pup.

I can't be a rabbit,

S O N G

So I'll be an Easter Ribbit.

It's true I'm green, but if I'm seen,

I really can ad-lib it.

I'll leave some Easter baskets,

And everyone will cheer.

A tisket, a tasket,

The Ribbit has been here!

And from that day to this, if you listen carefully you will always hear the little frogs called "peepers" singing in the woods in early spring. They are telling the story of Froggie the Easter Ribbit and how he became a hero to little frogs everywhere.

FROGGIE'S SONG

FROM THE PAGES OF
FRANKENSTEIN

"We are unfashioned creatures, but half made up."   (page 24)

Thus strangely are our souls constructed, and by such slight ligaments are we bound to prosperity or ruin.   (page 37)

So much has been done, exclaimed the soul of Frankenstein—more, far more, will I achieve: treading in the steps already marked, I will pioneer a new way, explore unknown powers, and unfold to the world the deepest mysteries of creation.   (page 42)

It was on a dreary night of November that I beheld the accomplishment of my toils. With an anxiety that almost amounted to agony, I collected the instruments of life around me, that I might infuse a spark of being into the lifeless thing that lay at my feet. It was already one in the morning; the rain pattered dismally against the panes, and my candle was nearly burnt out, when, by the glimmer of the half-extinguished light, I saw the dull yellow eye of the creature open; it breathed hard, and a convulsive motion agitated its limbs.   (page 51)

I thought I saw Elizabeth, in the bloom of health, walking in the streets of Ingolstadt. Delighted and surprised, I embraced her; but as I imprinted the first kiss on her lips, they became livid with the hue of death; her features appeared to change, and I thought that I held the corpse of my dead mother in my arms.   (page 51)

Did any one indeed exist, except I, the creator, who would believe, unless his senses convinced him, in the existence of the living monument of presumption and rash ignorance which I had let loose upon the world?   (page 72)

"You accuse me of murder; and yet you would, with a satisfied conscience, destroy your own creature. Oh, praise the eternal justice of man!"   (page 90)